Looking for Yesterday

Alison Jay

Old Barn Books

Yesterday was the best day.

I wish I could go back and do it all again.

But how?

I know when you look at the stars
you are looking at light from a million yesterdays.

I would need to go faster than light –

One hundred and eighty-six thousand miles per second...

over seven and a half times anti-clockwise

$V(x) = \int v_0$

$B = v_0$

$\sqrt{2mE}$

299792458 m/s

around the earth every second... to get back to yesterday.

What goes faster
than light?

A bus can't travel at superluminal speed.

or a super hypersonic rocket, or...

Some scientists say there are wormholes in space that could take us back in time...

I've just got to find one!

(and shrink myself to one billion, trillion, trillionth of a centimetre!)

Grandad, can you help me to find the way back to yesterday?

"Why do you want to go back to yesterday?

"Because it was the
best day Grandad!"

"Yesterday was a wonderful day, but there are many more happy days to come.

Let me tell you about some of my best days."

I have seen ten thousand birds fly through a sunset...
I have seen bright lights shimmer across a black sky...

I have danced by moonlight with the love of my life...
I have laughed until dawn with friends old and new.

I have floated through clouds...

and over thundering water.

I have climbed high to the top of a snow-capped mountain...

and dived deep beneath a blue ocean.

Our best days make happy memories,

But every day brings the chance of a new adventure.
Why go looking for yesterday when you can be happy here...

TODAY!